W9-CFK-442

Copyright © 1992 by Winston-Derek Publishers, Inc.

All rights reserved. No part of this book may be reproduced in any form without written permission from the publishers, except by a reviewer who may quote brief passages in a review to be printed in a newspaper or magazine.

First printing

PUBLISHED BY WINSTON-DEREK PUBLISHERS, INC.
Nashville, Tennessee 37205

Library of Congress Catalog Card No: 90-71855
ISBN: 1-55523-409-7

Printed in the United States of America

For Shirley Fay

GRINDING WHEAT INTO FLOUR

RUMPELSTILTSKIN

**Retold and Illustrated by
Fred Crump, Jr.**

TO SOW THE FALLOW SOIL

Winston-Derek Publishers, Inc.
Pennywell Drive—P.O. Box 90883
Nashville, TN 37209

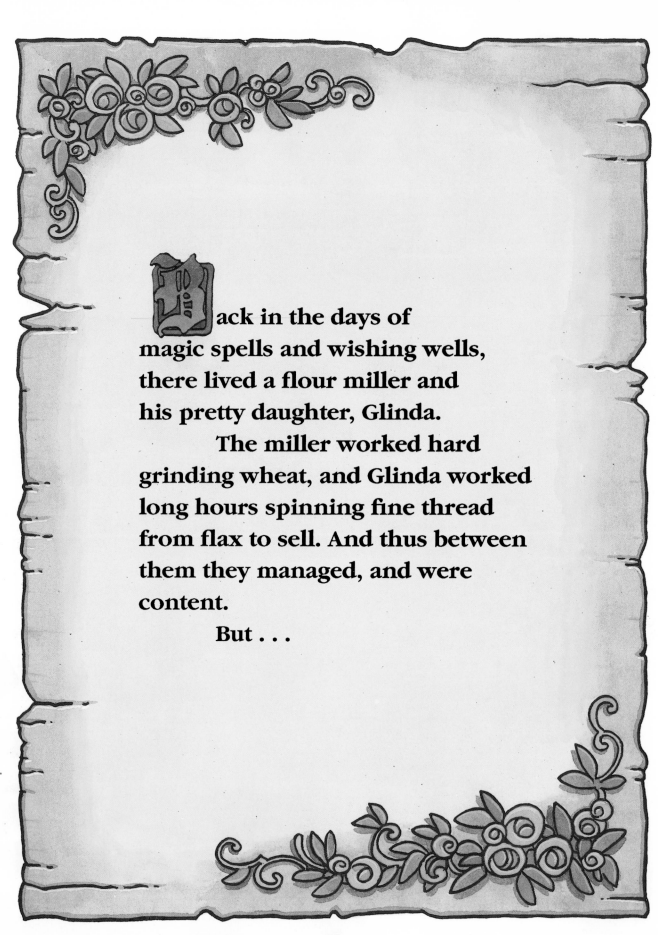

Back in the days of magic spells and wishing wells, there lived a flour miller and his pretty daughter, Glinda.

The miller worked hard grinding wheat, and Glinda worked long hours spinning fine thread from flax to sell. And thus between them they managed, and were content.

But . . .

SPINNING FLAX INTO THREAD

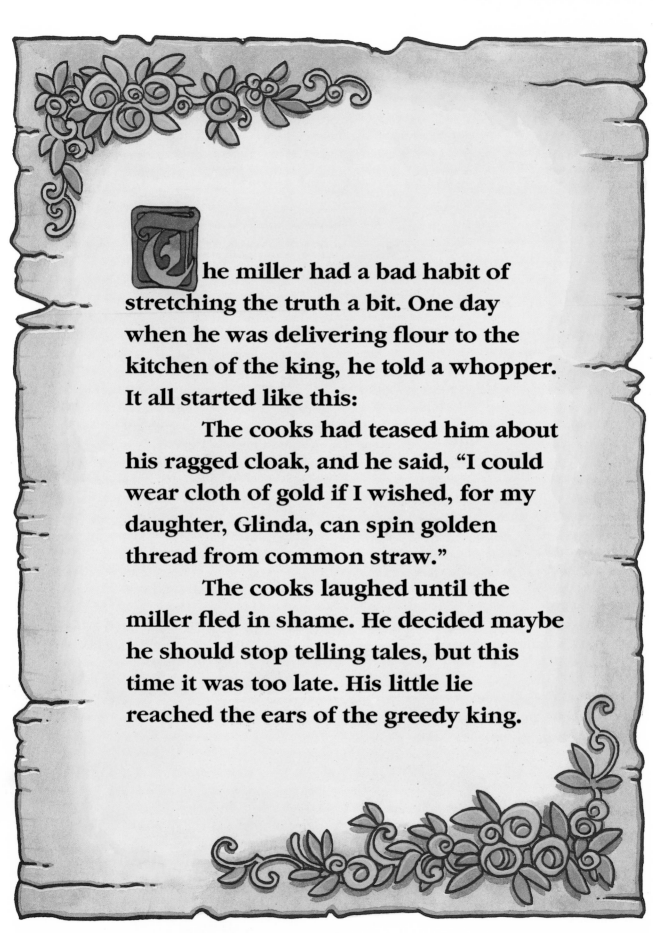

The miller had a bad habit of stretching the truth a bit. One day when he was delivering flour to the kitchen of the king, he told a whopper. It all started like this:

The cooks had teased him about his ragged cloak, and he said, "I could wear cloth of gold if I wished, for my daughter, Glinda, can spin golden thread from common straw."

The cooks laughed until the miller fled in shame. He decided maybe he should stop telling tales, but this time it was too late. His little lie reached the ears of the greedy king.

THE MILLER BRAGGED TOO MUCH

The king commanded, "Bring this magic spinner of golden thread to me at once!" Within the hour, Glinda was found and taken from her weeping father to the royal court.

She was very fearful as she entered the elegant throne room. The king was a frowning royal grouch. But his handsome son, Galen, welcomed her with a smile. Glinda blushed and smiled back.

"I wish to see this magic your father brags of," said the king. "I have a basket of straw and a spinning wheel in the dungeon. You will be kept there until you have spun twelve spindles of golden thread, be it one night or forever!"

Prince Galen tried to argue with the king, but it was useless. Glinda was taken to the dungeon.

GLINDA WAS A PRISONER

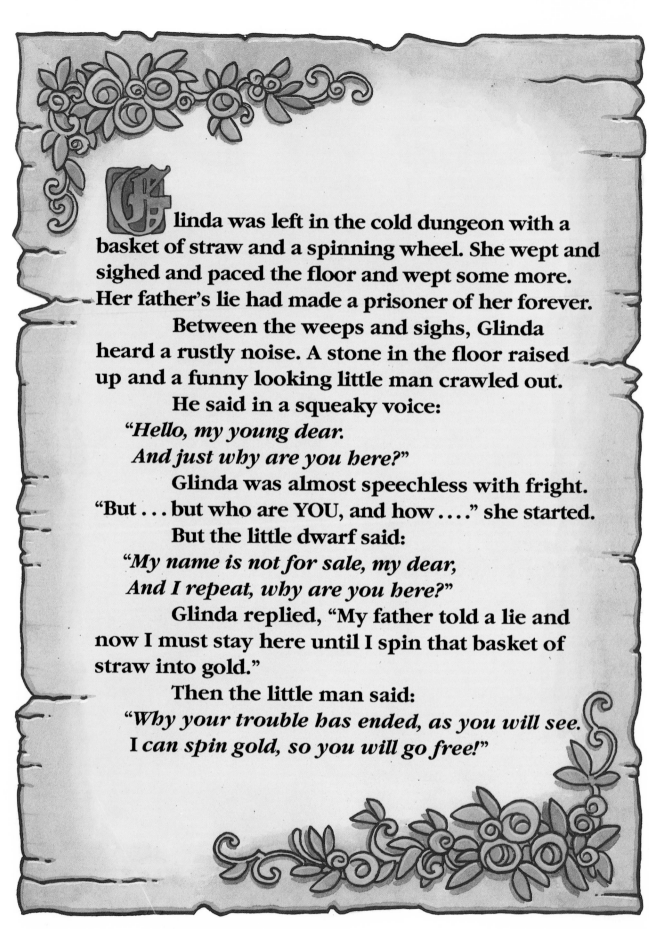

Glinda was left in the cold dungeon with a
basket of straw and a spinning wheel. She wept and
sighed and paced the floor and wept some more.
Her father's lie had made a prisoner of her forever.

Between the weeps and sighs, Glinda
heard a rustly noise. A stone in the floor raised
up and a funny looking little man crawled out.

He said in a squeaky voice:

"Hello, my young dear.
And just why are you here?"

Glinda was almost speechless with fright.
"But . . . but who are YOU, and how . . . ." she started.

But the little dwarf said:

"My name is not for sale, my dear,
And I repeat, why are you here?"

Glinda replied, "My father told a lie and
now I must stay here until I spin that basket of
straw into gold."

Then the little man said:

"Why your trouble has ended, as you will see.
I can spin gold, so you will go free!"

8

A STRANGE LITTLE MAN APPEARED

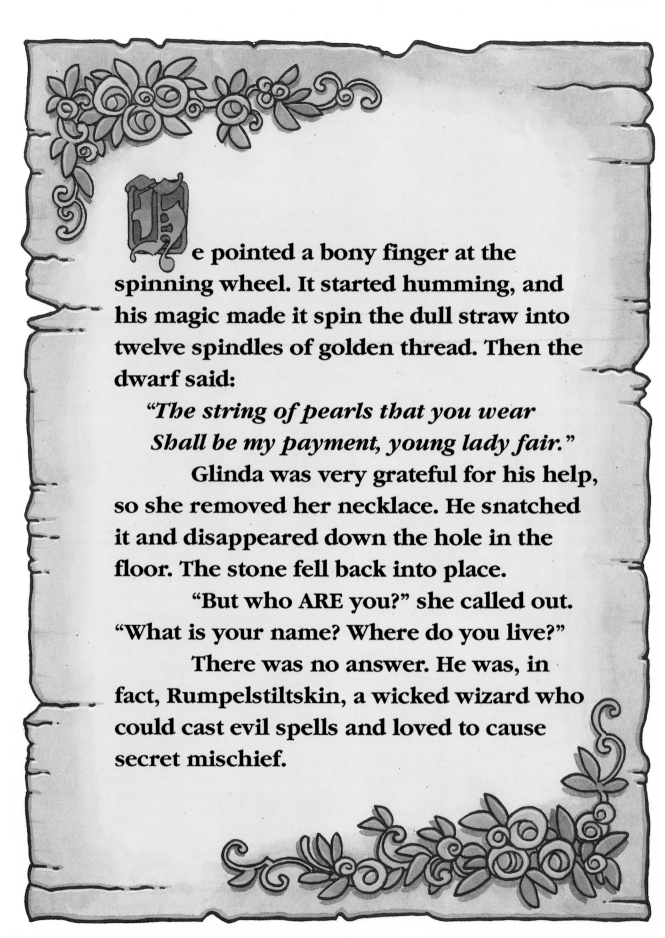

He pointed a bony finger at the spinning wheel. It started humming, and his magic made it spin the dull straw into twelve spindles of golden thread. Then the dwarf said:

"The string of pearls that you wear
Shall be my payment, young lady fair."

Glinda was very grateful for his help, so she removed her necklace. He snatched it and disappeared down the hole in the floor. The stone fell back into place.

"But who ARE you?" she called out. "What is your name? Where do you live?"

There was no answer. He was, in fact, Rumpelstiltskin, a wicked wizard who could cast evil spells and loved to cause secret mischief.

HE TURNED THE STRAW INTO GOLD

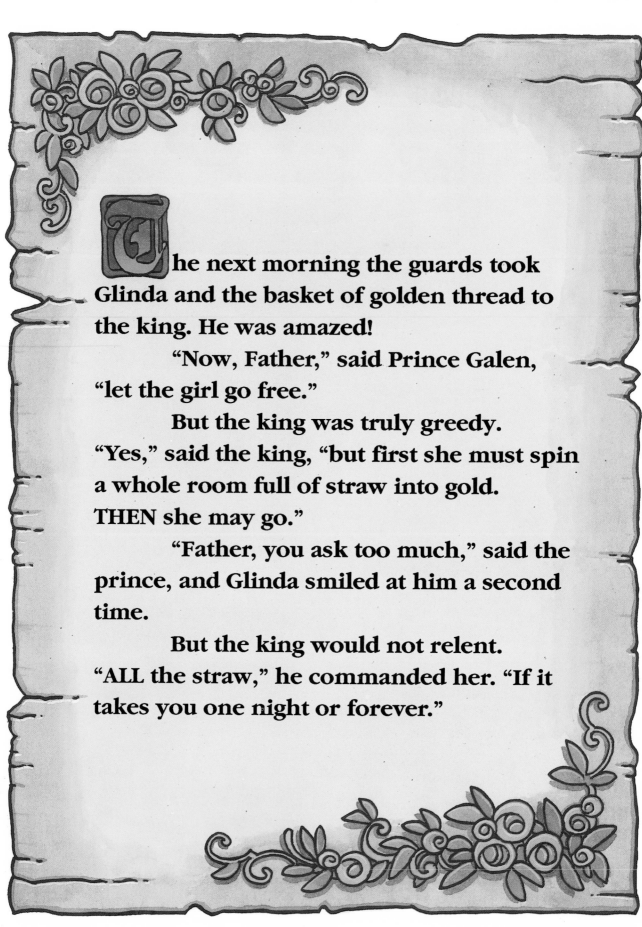

The next morning the guards took Glinda and the basket of golden thread to the king. He was amazed!

"Now, Father," said Prince Galen, "let the girl go free."

But the king was truly greedy. "Yes," said the king, "but first she must spin a whole room full of straw into gold. THEN she may go."

"Father, you ask too much," said the prince, and Glinda smiled at him a second time.

But the king would not relent. "ALL the straw," he commanded her. "If it takes you one night or forever."

THE GREEDY KING WANTED MORE

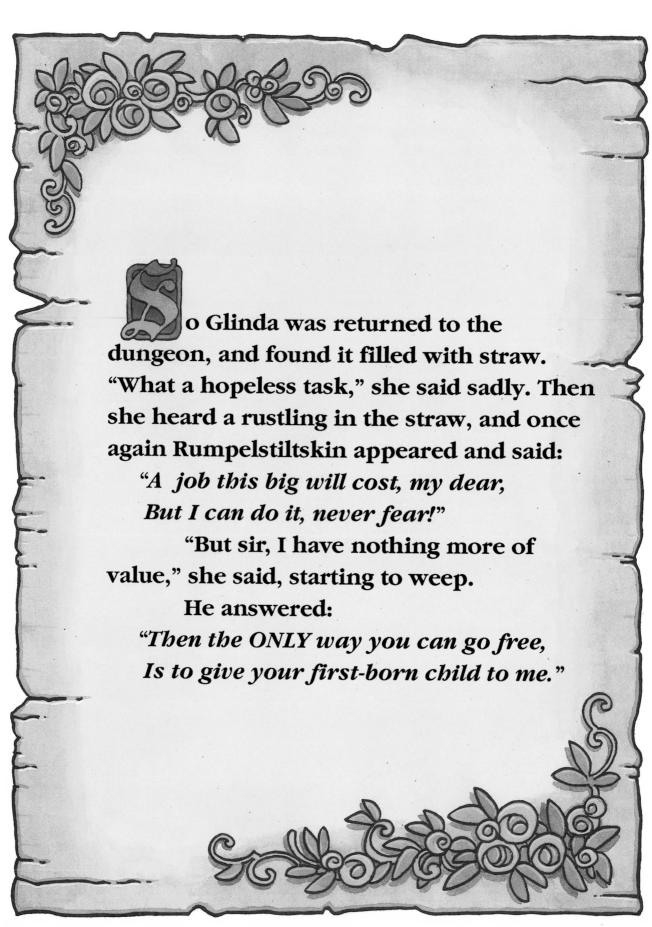

So Glinda was returned to the dungeon, and found it filled with straw. "What a hopeless task," she said sadly. Then she heard a rustling in the straw, and once again Rumpelstiltskin appeared and said:

"A job this big will cost, my dear,
But I can do it, never fear!"

"But sir, I have nothing more of value," she said, starting to weep.

He answered:

"Then the ONLY way you can go free,
Is to give your first-born child to me."

A DUNGEON FiLLED WiTH STRAW

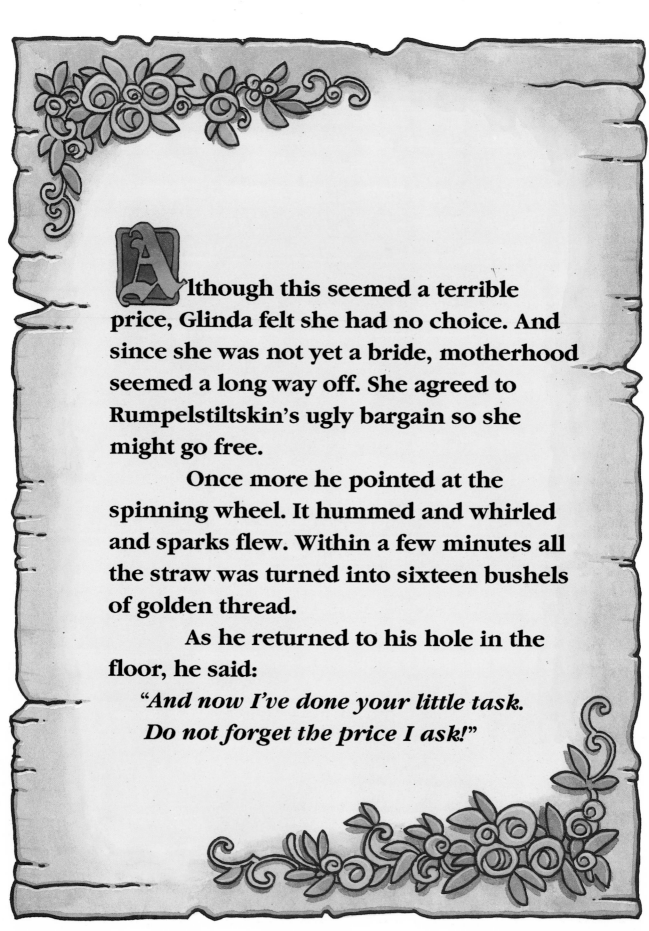

Although this seemed a terrible price, Glinda felt she had no choice. And since she was not yet a bride, motherhood seemed a long way off. She agreed to Rumpelstiltskin's ugly bargain so she might go free.

Once more he pointed at the spinning wheel. It hummed and whirled and sparks flew. Within a few minutes all the straw was turned into sixteen bushels of golden thread.

As he returned to his hole in the floor, he said:

"And now I've done your little task.
Do not forget the price I ask!"

SHE MADE A TERRIBLE PROMISE

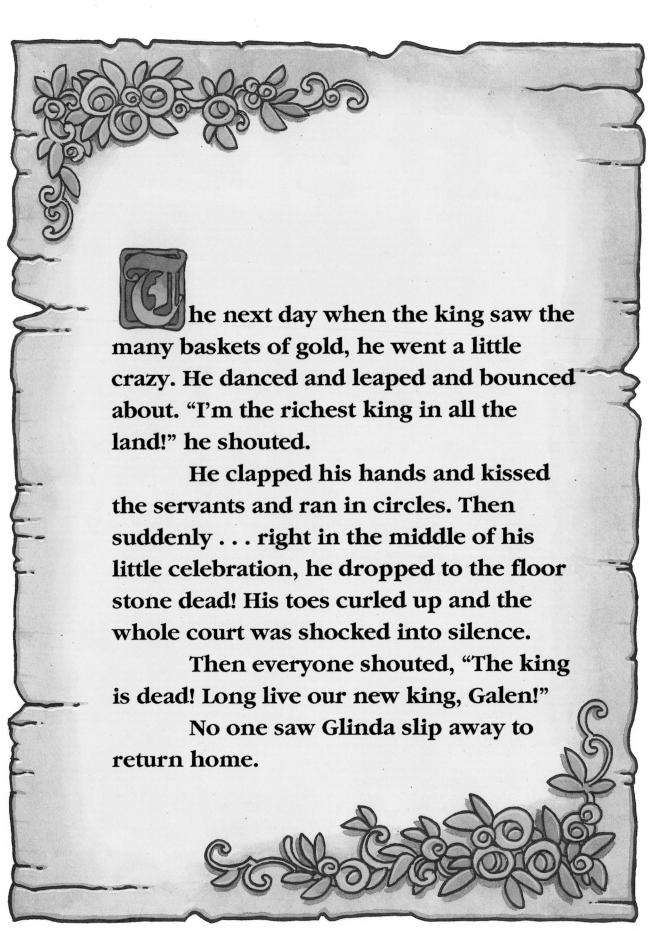

The next day when the king saw the many baskets of gold, he went a little crazy. He danced and leaped and bounced about. "I'm the richest king in all the land!" he shouted.

He clapped his hands and kissed the servants and ran in circles. Then suddenly . . . right in the middle of his little celebration, he dropped to the floor stone dead! His toes curled up and the whole court was shocked into silence.

Then everyone shouted, "The king is dead! Long live our new king, Galen!"

No one saw Glinda slip away to return home.

THE KiNG CELEBRATED TOO MUCH

After the royal funeral for the old king there was a thirty-day period of mourning. The kingdom was draped in black.

On the thirty-first day, young King Galen rode to the hut of the miller and asked for Glinda's hand in marriage.

Her happy smile was his answer. Then the black of the funeral gave way to the flowers of a most glorious wedding. The miller's daughter became a queen, and they lived happily until . . . .

THE MILLER'S DAUGHTER BECAME A QUEEN

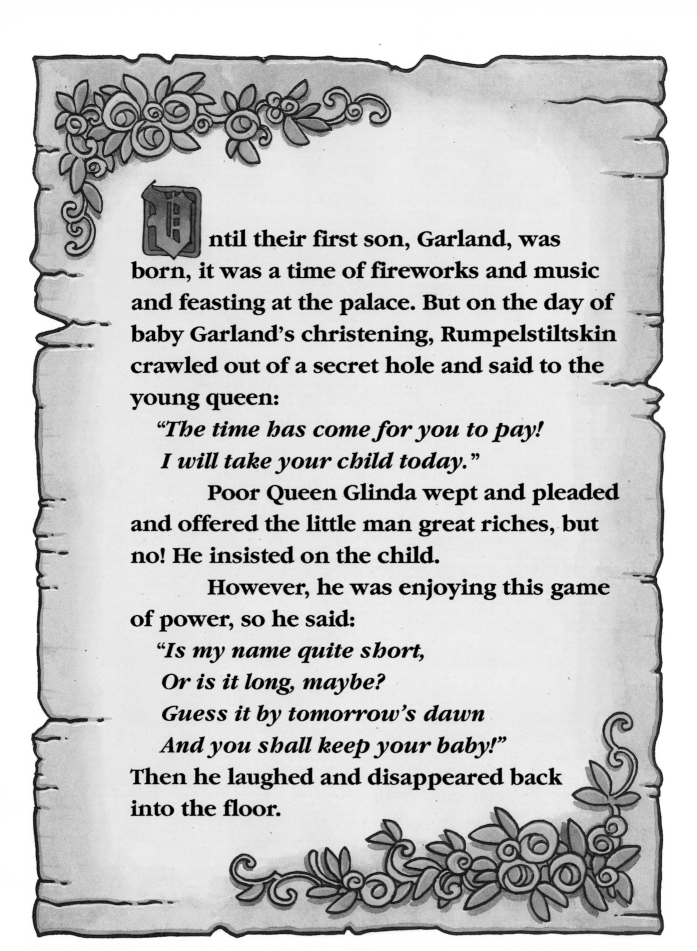

ntil their first son, Garland, was born, it was a time of fireworks and music and feasting at the palace. But on the day of baby Garland's christening, Rumpelstiltskin crawled out of a secret hole and said to the young queen:

"The time has come for you to pay!
I will take your child today."

Poor Queen Glinda wept and pleaded and offered the little man great riches, but no! He insisted on the child.

However, he was enjoying this game of power, so he said:

"Is my name quite short,
Or is it long, maybe?
Guess it by tomorrow's dawn
And you shall keep your baby!"

Then he laughed and disappeared back into the floor.

HE CAME TO TAKE THE BABY

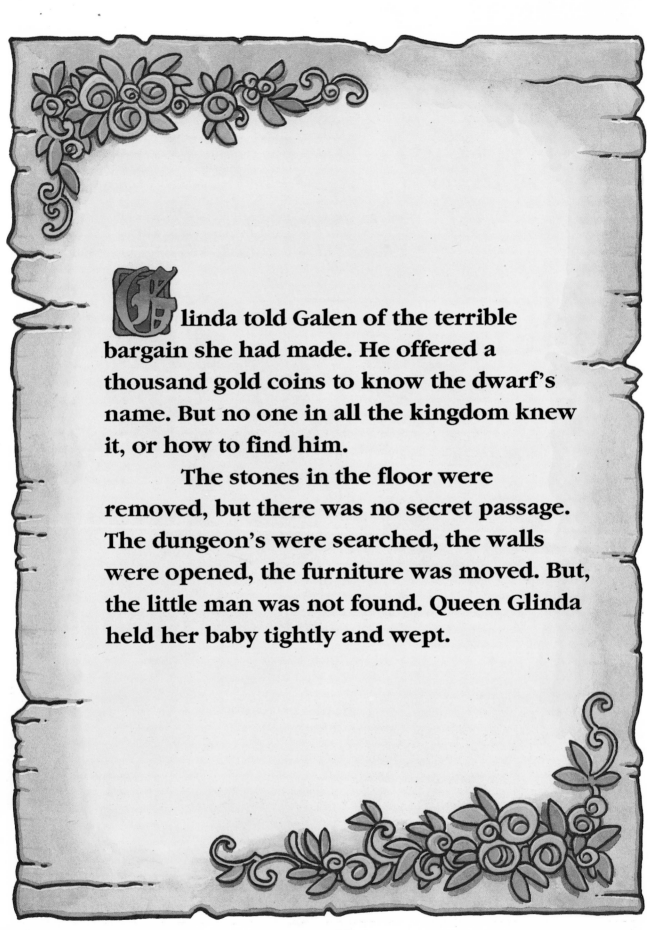

Glinda told Galen of the terrible bargain she had made. He offered a thousand gold coins to know the dwarf's name. But no one in all the kingdom knew it, or how to find him.

The stones in the floor were removed, but there was no secret passage. The dungeon's were searched, the walls were opened, the furniture was moved. But, the little man was not found. Queen Glinda held her baby tightly and wept.

THEY SEARCHED THE CASTLE

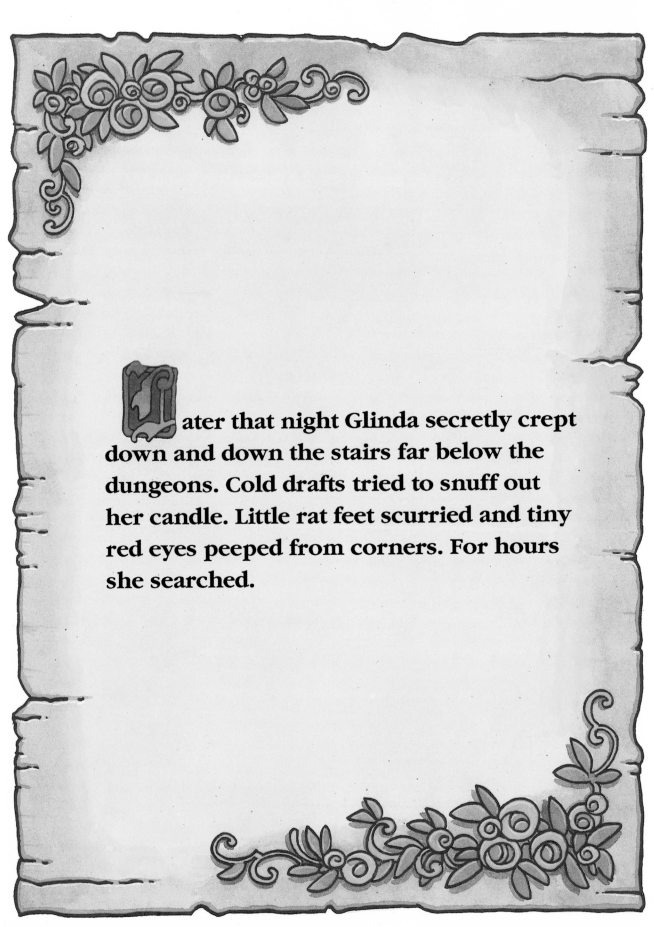

ater that night Glinda secretly crept down and down the stairs far below the dungeons. Cold drafts tried to snuff out her candle. Little rat feet scurried and tiny red eyes peeped from corners. For hours she searched.

SHE LOOKED FOR HOURS

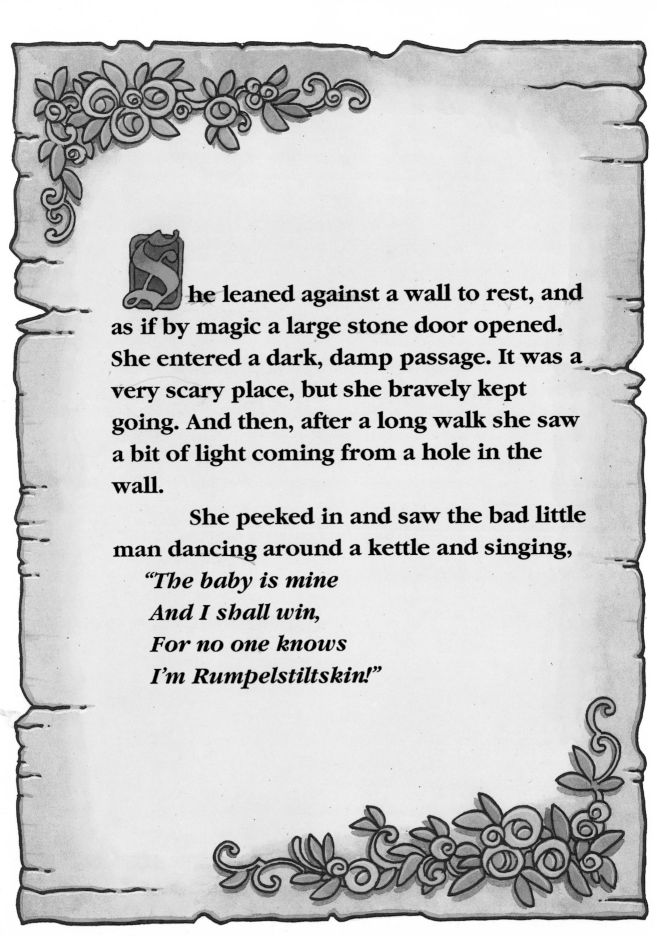

She leaned against a wall to rest, and as if by magic a large stone door opened. She entered a dark, damp passage. It was a very scary place, but she bravely kept going. And then, after a long walk she saw a bit of light coming from a hole in the wall.

She peeked in and saw the bad little man dancing around a kettle and singing,

"The baby is mine
And I shall win,
For no one knows
I'm Rumpelstiltskin!"

HE WAS SINGING

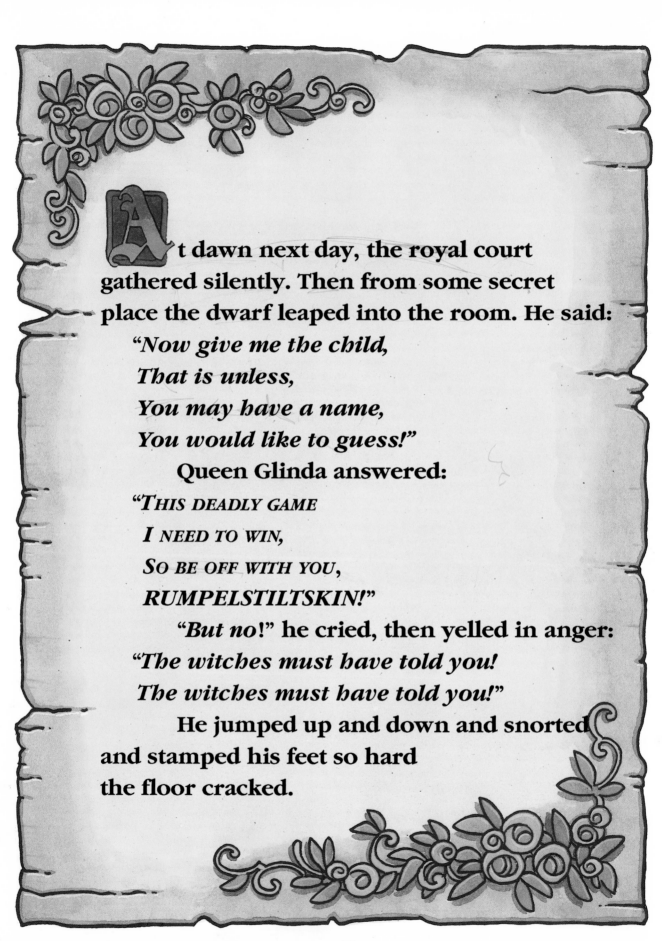

At dawn next day, the royal court gathered silently. Then from some secret place the dwarf leaped into the room. He said:

"*Now give me the child,*
That is unless,
You may have a name,
You would like to guess!"

Queen Glinda answered:

"*THIS DEADLY GAME*
I NEED TO WIN,
SO BE OFF WITH YOU,
RUMPELSTILTSKIN!"

"*But no!*" he cried, then yelled in anger:
"*The witches must have told you!*
The witches must have told you!"

He jumped up and down and snorted and stamped his feet so hard the floor cracked.

HE WAS VERY ANGRY

hen a hole opened in the floor and swallowed him up in a cloud of sparks and dust and rocks.

And that was the end of wicked Rumpelstiltskin.